www.mascotbooks.com

Football Freddie and Fumble the Dog: Gameday in Dallas

For more information, please contact:
Mascot Books
620 Herndon Parkway #320
Herndon, VA 20170
info@mascotbooks.com

Library of Congress Control Number: 2020901184

CPSIA Code: PRT0320A
ISBN-13: 978-1-64543-114-5

Printed in the United States of America

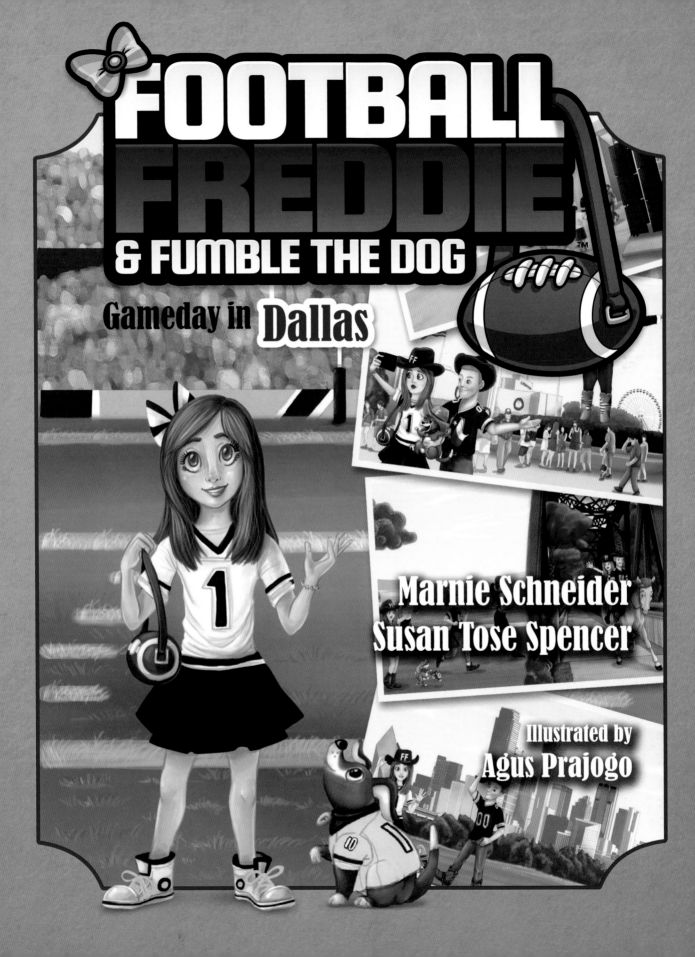

"There are no traffic jams along the extra mile."

– Roger Staubach, Dallas Cowboys Quarterback

Howdy! My name is Freddie, short for Fredericka, and this is my trusty companion, **Fumble**. We love everything about football: watching, playing, and most of all, traveling to different places where teams play their games. I started playing flag football in gym class, and soon I was throwing footballs for Fumble in my backyard—he's a great receiver!

Today, we're on our way to Dallas, Texas to watch the Cowboys play. Visiting the Big D, as locals call it, is one of the best ways to get to know the team and their fans. So, it's time to put on our boots and cowboy hats and find out if everything really IS bigger in Texas!

Fumble and I are really lucky, because my friend J.R. is going to be showing us around Dallas! He knows a lot about his hometown: the most delicious places to eat, the coolest landmarks to visit, and, of course, the best spots to throw a football. Maybe he'll even show us the proper way to wear a cowboy hat! The first cowboy hat was designed in 1865 by John B. Stetson, one of the most famous hat manufacturers in the world! It became known as the "Boss of the Plains" and has been a part of cowboy culture ever since!

Dallas is the third-largest city in Texas, which is saying a lot for a state as big as this one! It was founded by John Neely Bryan (and his dog!) in the mid-1800s. How Dallas got its name is still a mystery in the history books, but it didn't take long for the railroad to come into town and turn Dallas into one of the busiest places in Texas.

Dallas is home to no fewer than eight major league sports teams, which is pretty impressive for just one city! J.R. told us that football is super important to everyone here, but basketball, baseball, soccer, and even hockey boost the pride of all the sports fans in Dallas. And don't even get J.R. started on college football! He goes to the Red River Showdown, an annual college rivalry football game, every year with his family. This year, J.R.'s brother is attending the University of Texas at Austin, one of the competing colleges. **Go Longhorns!**

University of Texas at Dallas

Richland College

University of Dallas

Southern Methodist University

Dallas

Mountain View College

Paul Quinn College

Dallas Baptist University

University of North Texas at Dallas

High schools play their games on Friday nights—the origin of the term "Friday night lights"—but college players usually have their games on Saturday!

J.R. is starting our tour on the **Trinity River**, upon which Dallas was founded. If you follow the river all the way down the state, you get to the Gulf of Mexico. J.R. and I think that's a long swim, but Fumble thinks he can do it!

"Setting a goal is not the main thing. It is deciding how you will go about achieving it and staying with that plan."
-Tom Landry

While we're there, we see an armadillo on the shore! Armadillos are the official state animal of Texas—they're everywhere! Fumble was a little nervous at first, but they became fast friends. J.R. told us that armadillos can actually swim and cross rivers just like the Trinity. That must be really nice when it's hot (so, most of the time!).

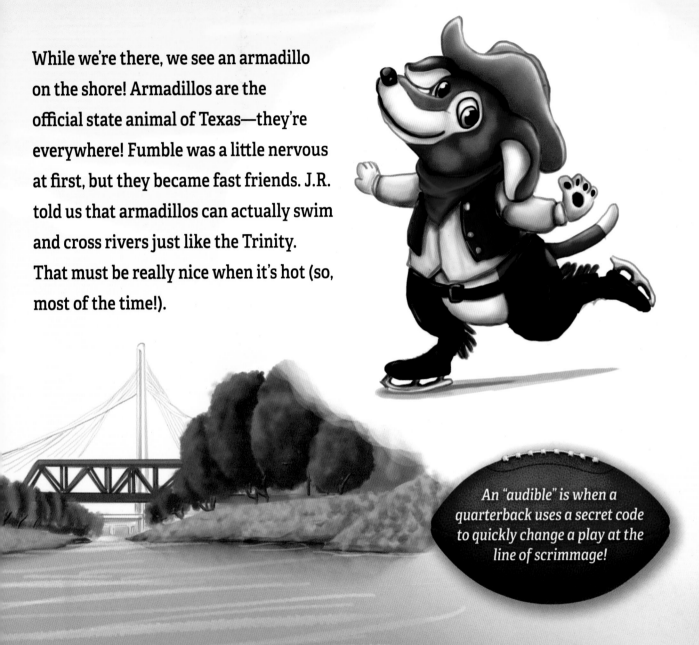

An "audible" is when a quarterback uses a secret code to quickly change a play at the line of scrimmage!

From our spot on the river, we can see the **Margaret Hunt Hill Bridge**. It's daytime now, but I bet it looks really cool when it's lit up at night! Underneath the bridge, a bunch of people are swimming in the water. J.R. says that Texans have come up with a lot of ways to beat the heat. They even have a special ice skating rink at the Dallas Galleria!

We head on over to another favorite watering hole in Dallas: **White Rock Lake**. This is one of the best places for boating and rowing, according to J.R. Fumble points out some people running around the lake, and we ask J.R. what they're up to. He tells us that they're practicing for the White Rock Marathon, which circles the lake. It seems like a lot of work, but we football fans know that hard work really pays off!

For a change of pace, J.R. introduces us to the **Katy Trail**. Fumble and I aren't prepared for the simple beauty of the bridges and tunnels left behind by railroad companies. People come here to hike, bike, and even ride on horseback!

Look at Fumble on his hobby horse! Did you know hobby horse racing is a big deal in Finland? Their national competition has over 400 competitors a year!

All of this walking and hiking is really giving us an appetite! J.R. takes us to his favorite restaurant, **Pecan Lodge**. It's famous in Dallas for its savory barbecue.

In fact, barbecue is so popular here, you can practically find it anywhere: on the street from vendors, at carnivals and fairs, and, of course, at every tailgate in the city! We couldn't come all this way not to try pulled pork and brisket. This is what they call a five napkin meal!

While barbecue is a true Texas staple, J.R. reminds us that chili, chicken fried steak, and sweet tea are also just as big of a deal. Since Texas is so close to Mexico, there is also a strong tradition of Mexican cuisine here. That's how we got the term "Tex-Mex," after all!

Football players are healthy eaters—and they eat A LOT! They're usually eating up until just a few hours before kickoff!

Now that our stomachs are full, it's time to head over to the arts district in Dallas, one of the most vibrant parts of the whole city. We'll have to move fast if we want to see everything! There's the **Dallas Museum of Art**, Nasher Sculpture Center, Meadows Museum, and the Winspear Opera House, to name just a few of the hubs of art and music. As we look at a huge Jackson Pollock painting hanging in the art museum, we can hear music coming from Deep Ellum nearby, which is famous for its rich history of jazz and blues—J.R.'s favorite music!

Close by is the Perot Museum, which has huge reproductions of dinosaur bones. Did you know that paleontologists from the museum discovered a new species of dinosaur?

Watch out, Fumble—those bones are a little too big for you! I guess everything really is bigger in Texas!

In the early days of football, instead of wearing helmets, players grew their hair really long and pinned it up to protect their heads!

Fumble is really excited for our next stop: the Dallas Zoo! He is so happy to see all of the animals that he starts barking up a storm! This is the largest and oldest zoo in Texas, and we make a point to find where the armadillos live! "They take really good care of their animals here!" J.R. says.

After the excitement of all of the zoo animals, J.R. takes us to a quiet spot in Dallas—the **John F. Kennedy Memorial**, constructed in honor of the president. Fumble and I take a few moments to remember him, with J.R. quoting John F. Kennedy: "Every accomplishment starts with the decision to try."

This is **Fair Park**, the host of the annual State Fair of Texas, held every year since 1886. Everyone is out in full Texas style, boots and all! There's pie eating contests, fireworks, and even live country music. Don't get too jealous of their dog show, Fumble! You're just as great as they are—you're our first round draft pick!!

Big Tex, the mascot of the fair, is always right in the middle of the action and towers over the crowd. It's easy to get lost in the middle of all there is to do, but Big Tex always guides the way home.

The sun is starting to sink closer to the ground, so J.R. takes us to the top of **Bank of America Plaza**, the tallest building in Dallas. From up here, we have an amazing view of the sunset and the Dallas skyline. The Ferris wheel in Fair Park looks so small! It's getting closer to game time, but J.R. says there's one more important place we have to visit.

Pioneer Plaza is a spot dedicated to the settlers that helped create modern Texas and is a tribute to the early days of Dallas's rich history. J.R. shows us the famous cattle drive sculptures created by Texas artist Robert Summers. Just like everything we've seen so far in Dallas, the cattle are larger than life! J.R. shows off his roping skills while we're there, and teaches us the best way to lasso!

We make our way to **AT&T Stadium**, where the home team plays. We're just in time for the tailgate. The fans are so friendly and treat us like their own! It takes a lot of work to host a football game. You need police, security, parking attendants, food vendors, cheerleaders, coaches, football players, ticket handlers, and the most important part—FANS! Everyone takes part in making the home team one of the most celebrated in the country!

Look at the cheerleaders! They're world-famous—some people come to games just to watch them perform! Cheering for others always makes you a leader.

When they start to play the National Anthem, all of us take off our cowboy hats. J.R. whispers that it is one of the most important rules when it comes to wearing cowboy hats: always remove them when our anthem is playing. Once we all take our seats, it's time for kickoff!

The team was first known as the Dallas Steers, then the Dallas Rangers. In 1960, they officially became the Cowboys.

Field goals earn you three points, which is half of a touchdown score!

After a tense first half, with the opposing team throwing a long pass, the home team still has the lead—but only by one point. Luckily, it's halftime, so we can all take a deep breath while we watch the celebrations down on the field.

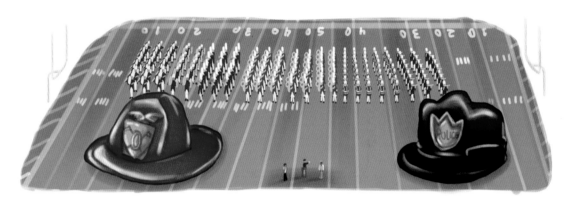

Today, Dallas is showing us what hometown pride is all about by showcasing their dedication to first responders and the military with a concert featuring veteran musicians. J.R.'s cousin is serving overseas, so this is a very special moment for us to share with J.R. When the players come back to the field, all of us are even more excited and ready to win!

The original cheerleading squad was made up of a male-female group called the "CowBelles & Beaux." The group made its sidelines debut in 1960 during the Cowboys' inaugural season.

Our opponents keep surprising us with some amazing long passes. In the end, Dallas closes out with a game-winning field goal. The stadium erupts in cheers, and we celebrate a really great game. That's Dallas for you—go big or go home!

Well, Fumble, looks like it's time to hang our hats and call it a day. J.R. has been an amazing host, sharing both his memories and his city with us. Football fans everywhere always know how to show us a good time, and Dallas is no exception. Before bed, we'll write a "thank you" note to J.R. for giving us a true Texas welcome. Manners matter!

XOXO *(that's football language)*,

– Football Freddie and
Fumble the Dog

About the Authors

A Pennsylvania native and Penn State graduate (WE ARE!), Marnie's life has been driven by sports. Her grandfather, Leonard Tose, was a longtime member of the "club" as the owner of the Philadelphia Eagles. He was also the founder of the Ronald McDonald House and helped build NFL Films. From him, Marnie learned the importance of family, sports, and charity. Her series, *Football Freddie and Fumble the Dog* is her way of giving back to the many great football communities across the nation.

Leonard Tose and the young author.

Susan T. Spencer was the first woman in pro football to be the vice president, legal counsel, and acting general manager. She did all of this at the Philadelphia Eagles. She's the author of *Briefcase Essentials* and co-author of *Gameday in Philadelphia*, the first book in the Football Freddie series. Susan also runs a very successful nonprofit called A Level Playing Field, which helps kids play sports safely.

Dallas Facts

Big things happen here

Flag

Year of Establishment

1841

Nicknames

*Big D, Metroplex, Triple D,
City of Hate, D-Town*

"My mother was the most beautiful woman I ever saw. All I am I owe to my mother. I attribute my success in life to the moral, intellectual, and physical education I received from her."

– George Washington

Dedicated to my mom,
Susan Tose Spencer, the best cheerleader
for me and my kids in the world!

The first ever female GM, Legal Counsel,
and VP of a pro football club!